DREW DROP
and the WATER CYCLE

Drew Drop and the Water Cycle

Written by Cathy Sherman

Illustrated by Ethan Kimberling

Copyright Date: October 2013

Printed by CreateSpace, An Amazon.com Company

ISBN: 978-1492282600

Dedicated to Jennifer and Josie,
my inspiration and helpful advisors

All streams flow into the sea,
yet the sea is never full.
To the place (from) which they flow,
the streams flow back again.

- Ecclesiastes 1:7 - JPS translation

At the ocean, water can be seen for miles and miles. Sometimes all that you can see are water and sky. Both the sea and the sky are made up of millions and millions of water drops and air. The water in the sea has more water and less air than the water in the sky. Each tiny drop of water can tell a different story of its life.

Right now, on any beach, waves may be washing the shore and splashing up against rocks that hug the shoreline. One little drop is riding a wave toward the beach at this very second!

Splash! Splat!

"Ouch, that hurts!" Drew looks around and tries to figure out just where he had landed. He looks for his friends, but cannot recognize any of the drops that landed with him.

Drew feels the warmth of the sun. "Oh-h-h here I go," he said. Whoosh! The sun's warmth is changing Drew into a smaller drop and causing him to float up and uP, and UP!

Drew starts singing and humming a new song, "What a wonderful day, and a wonderful way, to travel. Hum-m-m-m . . . It's a sunny sunny day to move out of the sea, and a perfect day to travel up in the sky." ♫ ♪

Drew looks down and sees a fantastic view. On one side is blue for miles and miles, and on the other side he sees tan sand dotted with green tuffs of sea grass and a few scraggly trees. Further back are lots of trees. In the middle, the shoreline is a wavy white line, snaking along the tan sand. He can see the big frothy splashes where the waves hit against rocks.

He remembers being here before, but, that was some time ago. He hopes he will see some of his friends again soon.

"Hi, what's your name?" he says to another drop traveling the same way.

"Hi, my name is Daisy".

"How did you get here?" asks Drew.

Daisy tells Drew how she had rained down a couple of days ago and stayed in a puddle since then. There were lots of other drops there. Then drops kept leaving except during the night when it cooled down and only a few left. When the sun came out, most of the drops that had stayed in the puddle drifted up.

"Oh, yeah, been there, done that", said Drew. "But this time I stayed with the same group of drops for awhile. Now I'm on my own again."

"Yes," says Daisy. "You get used to being in a family, but there is a time to be together, and a time to travel alone. Either way, we get to see the world."

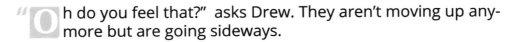"Oh do you feel that?" asks Drew. They aren't moving up anymore but are going sideways.

"Look, we are out over the ocean again!" he exclaims, not too happily. He really doesn't want to spend more time at sea right now. "Do you know if we are going east or west?"

"Oh we're going west," replies Daisy. "See, it's morning and the sun is at our backs."

There are islands down below, with lots of green trees, and palm trees. Drew wonders if there are banana trees, too. He likes bananas.

"Have you noticed that we're getting closer together?" Drew asks. Many more drops are gathering and they push against Drew and Daisy. But Drew gets caught in an updraft and has to say good-bye to Daisy.

T oo bad, Daisy was so nice. Drew is feeling very crowded now. It's getting cloudy, and he can't see the sun anymore. It's also getting dark. So he decides to curl up between two other drops and go to sleep.

"Hello Hello! Wake up will you! We are starting to move up faster, and I can't keep pushing a sleeping blob," says a loud voice which wakes Drew from a good dream.

"Oh, sorry. My name is Drew. Who are you?" he says.

"I'm Donny. Whew, it's much easier when I don't have to push."

"I must have dropped off for awhile. What time is it?"

"Who worries about time?" answers Donny. "We're getting ready to hit the coastland and we will be falling pretty soon, so that's the only time I care about. A time to fall, a time to rise, a time to . . ." he sings. ♪ ♫♪ ♫

"Oh yes, time to fall again. Where are we?" asks Drew.

"Boy do you ask the questions!" exclaims Donny. "Haven't you been this way before?"

"Well, I have been spending a lot of time in the ocean, and finally the wave I was riding got splashed on a rock on the shore. It has been awhile, and I guess I forgot," says Drew.

Donny doesn't know the names of the land. He had seen big stretches of flat land, islands, rivers and the ocean. Now they are heading toward a mountain. But they don't have any maps to tell them the names of the different parts of the land and water they are seeing. Donny just remembers the looks of each place and is happy with that. He doesn't need names. But names would make it easier to explain to Drew where they are.

onny sings his favorite song about bouncing. "I love to bounce on roofs and rocks, ♪ ♫ Oh so bouncy roofs and rocks, oh so smooth and never shocks, when you bounce on roofs and rocks . . ."

"Hey, have you been in a lake before?" interrupts Drew.

"Yes. I've been in many lakes. Some were big ones that a drop could get lost in for many years. Then there were the small lakes, where you could be in the middle and see the shore all around you. I can see for miles and miles and miles," sings Donny.

"I hope I can land in a lake, because I'm tired of the taste of salt. Say, Donny, do you always sing?" Donny nods his agreement. Then Drew begins to drop down, so that the other drops become lighter and can move up and go over the mountain.

"See ya-a-a-a-a-!" yells Drew.

Drew feels heavier and begins to fall faster. And right before him is the mountain. But instead of bumping into it, some of the drops continue over the top, and Drew lands on its side.

Splash! "Oh wow! Look at all the other drops. Whoa, we are moving fast!" says Drew, as he's caught in the flow of drops rushing down the mountain.

Drew asks a new drop next to him, "What are we in?"

"his is a stream," answers the new drop. "Do you know streams?"

"I've heard of them. So where are we going?"

"Down the mountain. Boy you ask a lot of questions."

"I know. Thanks for being patient with me."

"That's ok. It's good to be patient. Every storm soon passes, right? Oh, by the way, my name is Serena."

"Sure. I've had my share of storms. Oh look, Serena, did you see that pretty beach? Hey, what kinds of fish are these? And my name is Drew, in case I haven't already told you."

Serena knows that most of the fish have fins on their backs and tails. She describes to Drew some of the colors and shapes of fish in the oceans. Not all of the ocean fish have fins, but most of the river fish do.

Drew tells Serena about the huge fish he had seen in the ocean that spewed water out of a spout on the top of its head. She tells him that this fish is not really a fish, but a whale. She had heard stories of drops getting caught in the whale's mouth and spending time in his dark stomach. Finally they were sprayed out, to their relief and happiness. It had been really hard to be kept in the dark without seeing the sun for so long.

Drew, having never been swallowed by a whale, thinks the part about being sprayed out might be fun. But the thought of not seeing the sun for a few days makes him sad.

He goes on to tell Serena of some of his other fish sightings.

"I also saw a fish with a sword for a nose, and these other fish with sharp teeth. I tried to stay away from those fish."

"Just wait until we get down to the mouth of the river! We'll be sent into a lake or an ocean, where we just might see more colorful fish."

They're moving fast again. Some of the drops begin hitting rocks and flying up. Drew decides to stay away from rocks, because he wants to go to the lake.

He is sleepy again. "Wake me when we get there," he yells to no drop in particular.

When Drew wakes up, he's in the middle of a huge puddle, or what other drops call a lake. He knows it isn't the ocean, because it's not salty.

Drew feels a current in the lake and realizes he won't be staying here long.

He greets a different form of drop, whose name is Snowy. This whitish flake is happy to be warming up, even if it is causing his whiteness to change to a watery clearness. He tells about having been on top of a mountain for a long time.

"Did you come down as a snowflake?" asks Drew.

"Yes, how did you guess? I froze for what seemed like forever. It was so cold, not many drops were going up, but almost every day, more came down. I was buried for a long time but just slept through it. What about you? Where've you been?"

Before Drew can tell the new drop about his ocean adventures, he begins to feel a pull and realizes he's being sucked down. It's dark, but he sees a light up ahead.

"Where are we?" he yells. But Snowy goes a different way where he can't see him.

"We're in an irrigation pipe, silly. Haven't you seen one before?"

The new voice comes from a drop named Hailee. She had come down as an icy drop and had landed in a river. She seems to be excited about going into the irrigation ditch, though Drew cannot imagine why.

"Why, what happens in one of these …ir- ri -gay -shun ditches?" he asks as they flow out of the pipe and into a ditch.

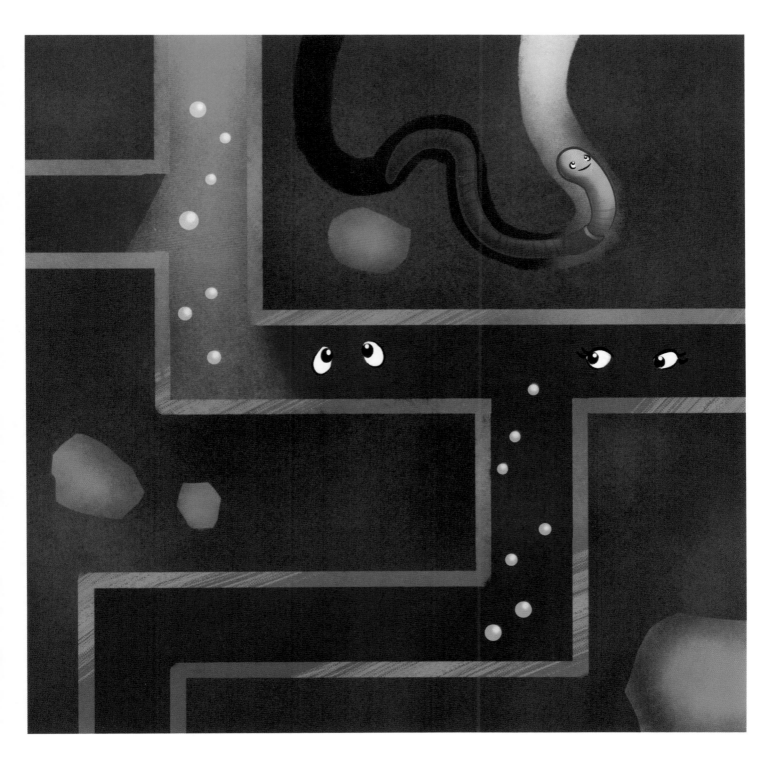

Hailee tells how they could get to go into a sprinkler and be sprayed out onto the ground. Some of them could get to go into a plant root and become part of a fruit, vegetable or flower.

She explains how others go down further into the ground and eventually end up in a well or underground spring.

When the drops get pushed though bits of rock and sand, they get cleaned. By the time the drops reach a well or a reservoir, the water is ready for drinking. There are many other ways water is used by people too.

Other drops which sprinkle out never even touch the ground. They are evaporated and go up into the air again.

"Wow," says Drew, "you sure know a lot, Hailee."

"I have traveled a lot," Hailee replies. "I don't think there is anywhere I haven't been. I can tell you lots of stories. There are lots of things that can happen and lots of ways of leaving this ditch."

"Well, thanks Hailee, for telling me about irrigation," says Drew. "There's so much in this world I don't know! Every day, I see and learn more."

"Well, gotta go – see ya!" And Hailee is off down another black tube.

D rew moves into another tube, but not for long.

All of a sudden, Drew has to blink because he's out in the blinding light once again, as the sprinkler shoots him out.

Other drops are going everywhere! He wonders if he will go up in a cloud again or fall back to the ground.

He doesn't have long to wonder though, as he falls splish-splash into the middle of a puddle. He is hoping to float and relax for a bit, but is startled by a four-legged critter running by.

"Hey, who are you? What are you? What are you doing?" Drew yells to the animal.

Drew figures this must be a dog. He has heard of dogs before. Now the dog is enjoying splashing the drops every direction in the air. Drew is stuck on the dog. He has to hold on tight because he doesn't want to be thrown off.

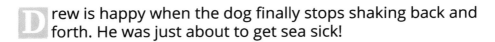rew is happy when the dog finally stops shaking back and forth. He was just about to get sea sick!

Then he starts to relax while he hitchhikes on this dog, but that doesn't last long either. Some kids come and start petting the dog.

"Hey watch out, don't squish me!" he yells.

Too late. They wipe Drew off and now he finds himself going up in the air again. It isn't so bad, because the dog is muddy and smelly anyway.

"Now what new adventure will I get to go on next?" Drew wonders.

"Mr. Mr. . . ." A small voice comes from a tiny droplet near Drew.

"Hello little one. How can I help you?" says Drew.

"I just got separated from my family. What's going to happen to me?"

"Oh not to worry. You will have many adventures, meet many new friends, but one thing is for sure."

"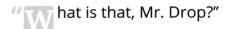hat is that, Mr. Drop?"

"As a drop, you will never, ever end, because drops don't end. You might take on many shapes, colors and sizes, cling to many kinds of dust and rocks, do a lot of climbing and falling, go through dark and sunny places, cold and hot places, but you'll never ever quit being a drop. And keep asking those questions."

"Wow, you know a lot."

"Yes, I have done my share of traveling," Drew says with a sigh.

The End

...there is no end...

Made in the USA
San Bernardino, CA
10 November 2013